Rachel Carson

Founder of the Environmental Movement

George Shea

BLACKBIRCH PRESS

An imprint of Thomson Gale, a part of The Thomson Corporation

Detroit • New York • San Francisco • San Diego • New Haven, Conn.
Waterville, Maine • London • Munich

Picture credits: Timelife Pictures/Getty Images, cover; AFP/Getty Images, 58; AP/Wide World Photos, 35, 54, 56; © Bettmann/CORBIS, 8, 45; Courtesy of the Lear/Carson Collection, Connecticut College/Carson Family photograph, 11; Courtesy of Chatham College, 13, 15; © David Muench/CORBIS, 10; © Earth Satellite Corporation/Photo Researchers, Inc., 23; Getty Images, 26–27, 51, 52; Jon Davison/Lonely Planet Images, 39; © Mary Frye/Rachel Carson Council , 17; National Geographic/Getty Images, 30; © Photo Researchers, Inc., 21 (inset); Photodisc, 32, 37; © Rachel Carson Council, 9, 21, 41; © Ralph White/CORBIS, 33; Suzanne Santillan, 48; © The Mariners' Museum/CORBIS, 24; Time Life Pictures/Getty Images, 5, 12; U.S. Fish & Wildlife Service, 36; U.S. Department of Agriculture, 6.

LIBRARY OF CONGRESS CATALOGING-IN-PUBLICATION DATA

Shea, George.
  Rachel Carson / by George Shea.
    p. cm. — (Giants of science)
  Includes bibliographical references and index.
  ISBN 1-4103-0568-6 (hardcover : alk. paper)
  1. Carson, Rachel, 1907–1964—Juvenile literature. 2. Biologists—United States—Biography—Juvenile literature. 3. Environmentalists—United States—Biography—Juvenile literature. I. Title. II. Series.

  QH31.C33S44 2005
  570'.92—dc22

                                                    2005001843

Printed in the United States of America
10 9 8 7 6 5 4 3 2 1

CONTENTS

Death from the Skies

In January 1958, Rachel Carson received a disturbing letter in her Silver Spring, Maryland, home. It read:

> The mosquito control plane flew over our small town last summer. . . . The "harmless" shower bath killed seven of our lovely songbirds outright. We picked up three dead bodies the next morning right by the door. They were birds that had lived close to us, trusted us, and built their nests in our trees year after year. The next day, three were scattered around the bird bath. I had emptied it and scrubbed it after the spraying but YOU CAN NEVER KILL DDT. On the following day, one robin dropped suddenly from a branch in our woods. We were too heartsick to hunt for other corpses. All of these birds died horribly, and in the same way. Their bills were gaping open, and their splayed claws were drawn up to their breasts in agony.[1]

Rachel Carson was deeply upset when she put down the letter. Its author, Olga Huckins, and her husband were Carson's friends. They had a bird sanctuary near their home on Cape Cod in Massachusetts. Now most, if not all, of their precious songbirds were dead.

Rachel Carson, shown here bird-watching in the woods of Maryland, dedicated her life to the study of nature and the impact of human activities on the environment.

A Desire to Take Action

All her life, Carson had been concerned about nature and the ways in which human beings selfishly or ignorantly kill harmless animals and damage the environment. She knew she had to do something to stop DDT and the spraying of fields, woods, and farmlands from the air with powerful and lethal chemicals. "Everything that meant most to me as a naturalist was being threatened,"[2] she wrote later.

Another friend of Carson's, ornithologist Robert Cushman Murphy, was a plaintiff in a lawsuit against the federal government. His home and thousands of acres of homes, farmlands, and other property on Long Island had been sprayed with deadly insecticides. Murphy and other Long Island residents were suing the federal government, which had ordered the spraying, because they believed their rights as private citizens had been violated by the spraying.

DDT, the "Miracle" Pesticide

Rachel Carson had long been aware of the dangers posed by DDT, which had been widely used since 1939. It was generally believed to be powerful and effective in killing mosquitoes and harmful insects that destroyed crops. During World War II, when South Pacific islands were invaded by American troops, DDT was used to clear those islands of mosquitoes that spread

malaria and other diseases. By 1945 and the end of World War II, many people regarded it as a miraculous way to eliminate harmful insect pests. Some people compared it to the atomic bomb, which had just been dropped on the Japanese cities of Hiroshima and Nagasaki, as a potent way to quickly wipe out insect pests that threatened humanity. Some government officials honestly believed it could be used to eradicate all the harmful insects on Earth. The U.S. government permitted the unrestricted purchase and use of DDT. Anyone could buy and use as much of the deadly chemical as he or she wanted.

No one seemed to be worried that, in addition to killing insects, DDT could also kill other forms of life and cause serious illnesses in humans. Moreover, like atomic radiation, DDT lasted for many years once it got into soil and groundwater or the bodies of human beings.

For more than ten years, Rachel Carson had been concerned about the problem. As early as 1945 she had tried to warn people about the toxic effects of DDT. She had proposed an article about the dangerous chemical compound to the *Reader's Digest*, but the magazine chose not to publish it.

Twelve years later, DDT and other dangerous chemicals seemed to be everywhere at once. A massive government program had been set up to wipe out the fire ant in the southern states. In truth, the fire ant was little more than a minor

A crop duster plane flies low to the ground as it sprays a cloud of DDT over rows of crops.

7

In this photo from 1945, a woman sprays DDT directly over her child.

nuisance and did no harm to crops. Yet 40 million acres (16 million hectares), an area larger than the state of Georgia, was sprayed with a solution that contained dieldrin, a pesticide 40 times more poisonous than DDT. People were heartbroken when they saw the corpses of thousands of songbirds, wild turkeys, quail, opossums, and raccoons throughout the area. Dogs, cats, chickens, cows, horses, and other farm animals sickened and died as well.

Government officials had made it clear they would not stop the spraying programs. If anything, they had plans to considerably increase them. The officials said they believed the insecticides had no bad side effects. They maintained that after the chemicals did their jobs, they simply disappeared. The government had no plans to do research to find out what the further effects of massive sprayings might be.

Sounding an Alarm

These policies deeply troubled Rachel Carson. She was a dedicated naturalist who believed that all the elements of life were connected. She knew humans could not damage or kill one part of an ecosystem without affecting all the other parts. She decided to personally investigate the spraying programs. She telephoned and wrote letters to witnesses who testified in the Long Island spraying trial. She also contacted scientists and government officials, as well as associates in conservation organizations and former colleagues from her years in government service. The more she found out, the more concerned she became. She knew she had to sound an alarm to wake up the country. *Silent Spring,* the book she published four years later in 1962, turned out to be one of the most influential books ever written. It forever changed the way human beings saw the planet on which they lived.

Family Life

Rachel Louise Carson was born very early on the morning of May 27, 1907, in her family's home in Springdale, Pennsylvania. She was the youngest of three children born to Robert and Maria Mclean Carson. Rachel's mother was 38 years old. Rachel's father was 43. He spent long periods of time away from home selling insurance. Her older sister, Marian, was 10 and in the fifth grade at the local elementary school. Her brother, Robert, was 8 and in the first grade.

Rachel Carson, shown here sitting on her mother Maria's lap, had two siblings: Marian (left) and Robert (right).

In 1900, when the Carsons first moved to Springdale, it was a growing community and a pleasant place to live. New industries were expected to move into the area. Robert Carson reasoned that people would want to build homes in Springdale. He decided to take a gamble and took a large mortgage on a scenic piece of property located on what is known as the Allegheny Bend. On the land was a small clapboard house with four small rooms into which the Carson family moved. The Allegheny River flowed nearby and boats went up and down the river carrying iron ore, oil, and lumber to nearby Pittsburgh, only eleven miles away.

Rachel grew up in Pennsylvania's lush Allegheny River Valley, where she developed a deep love of nature.

Carson's plan was to make money by selling off plots of the land. But his gamble never paid off. Few of the lots sold, and he often found it difficult to meet the payments on the mortgage. Nor did Robert Carson receive a regular salary from his employer. Instead, he was paid a percentage of his insurance sales, and he was not a successful salesman.

Rachel's mother was better educated than her husband. Maria had graduated with honors in Latin from the Washington Female Seminary in 1887 and took advanced courses at Washington College. After graduating, she taught school and gave private piano lessons. She met Robert Carson in 1893. A year later they married, and Maria gave up her teaching job because at that time married women were not permitted to work as teachers. She was an intelligent woman with a powerful and dominating personality, and an avid reader with strong intellectual interests.

Early Curiosity About Nature

One of her deepest interests was nature study, and she particularly enjoyed bird-watching. Her husband's absences and her elder children's daily school attendance gave Maria Carson and her younger daughter lots of time to take long, lazy walks around the family property. Maria Carson encouraged her children to love and respect all wild creatures. One of little Rachel's favorite pastimes was to give names to the flowers, birds, and insects they encountered. Years later, she wrote that she was always "happiest with wild birds and creatures as companions."[3]

Rachel also had a strong scientific curiosity. One day she was fascinated by a large seashell fossil she found. She wanted to know all about the seashell—how it had been formed, what sort of animal had made it and lived in it, and what the world had been like millions of years ago when a huge sea covered what was now western Pennsylvania.

As Rachel grew up, she watched unhappily as Springdale began to change and in some ways resemble the industrial city of Pittsburgh, which was notorious for being grimy and dirty. A glue factory that gave off foul smells was built in Springdale near the railway station. The beautiful Allegheny began to turn yellow as it filled up with the pollution that flowed downriver from Pittsburgh. Two huge power plants that were built at opposite ends of the little town squeezed the town

As a young girl, Rachel learned to name the many flowers and animals she encountered on her frequent walks.

Factories in Pittsburgh (pictured) polluted the Allegheny River downstream from Springdale, Rachel's childhood home.

between them and made it dreary and dirty. Watching this happen was a sad experience that Rachel never forgot.

A Student and Writer

Despite her sadness at the town's decline, Rachel enjoyed school and was an excellent student. At an early age, she showed natural promise as a writer. When she was ten, she entered a story in a contest sponsored by the prestigious *St. Nicholas Magazine*, the best-known children's magazine of the day. Her brother's service in the Army Air Corps during World War I inspired her first story, "A Battle in the Clouds." The story won a ten-dollar prize, a silver badge, and publication in the magazine. She submitted two more stories, and her third won an even bigger prize, a gold badge. Years later, in a speech to a group of women, she said, "I can remember no time, even in earliest childhood, when I didn't assume I was going to be a writer."[4]

Rachel got excellent grades in high school and graduated first in her class in May 1925. The following poem accompanied her class picture in the school yearbook:

Rachel's like the mid-day sun
Always very bright
Never stops her studying
'til she gets it right.[5]

Despite its humorous tone, the poem accurately described Rachel Carson. She was a diligent student who never gave up on anything.

Going to College

Although Rachel had excellent grades and wanted very badly to go to college, her family was too poor to pay her first year's board and tuition. Help arrived from the Pennsylvania College for Women (PCW), a highly regarded private college in Pittsburgh, which offered her a partial scholarship. Rachel then was awarded another scholarship from the State of Pennsylvania.

Rachel entered PCW with the goal of becoming a professional writer, an aspiration her freshman composition teacher, Grace Croff, was eager to encourage. Croft saw Rachel as the star of her English class and encouraged her to write for both the student newspaper, the *Arrow*, and the literary supplement, the *Englicode*. All through 1925 and 1926, Rachel and her teacher often sat

In 1925 Rachel enrolled in the Pennsylvania College for Women with the intention of becoming a writer.

together, deep in conversation on one of the wooden benches that dotted the campus.

A Story About the Sea

Croff's encouragement paid off when Rachel's story "The Master of the Ship's Light" was selected for publication in the *Englicode* during her freshman year. It was a story that took place on the ocean and the seacoast, two places Rachel had visited only in books and in her imagination. And yet she made the ocean scenes come alive for her readers. Croff praised the story highly and in a note to Rachel wrote: "Your style is so good because you have made what might be a relatively technical subject very intelligible to the reader."[6]

Her readers were surprised when they learned that Rachel had never been to the ocean. But she had always felt a kinship with it and recalled the thrill she felt when, late one night in the middle of a thunderstorm, she first read Alfred Lord Tennyson's poem "Locksley Hall," which contains the line, "For the mighty wind arises, roaming seaward, and I go."

"The more clearly we can focus our attention on the wonders and realities of the universe about us, the less taste we shall have for the destruction of our race. Wonder and humility are wholesome emotions, and they do not exist side by side with a lust for destruction."
—Rachel Carson

Years later, she wrote, "that line spoke to something within me, seeming to tell me that my own path led to the sea . . . and that my own destiny was somehow linked with the sea."[7]

Rachel was a serious young person who greatly valued her own solitude and intellectual independence. She had a considerable amount of natural reserve, a habit acquired from years of living in near poverty on the lonely family acreage in Springdale, where she had few friends. Some of her college classmates

Although Carson (top row, second from right) was a serious student at PCW, she made time to play on the school's field hockey team.

formed the opinion that she was conceited. But that was not true. She befriended a number of teachers and students—especially those who shared her interests in writing and nature. She had a good sense of humor and liked to spend time with the friends she had. She even played substitute goalie on the school's field hockey team all four of her years at PCW.

A Turning Point

To no one's surprise, when Carson had to select a major at the start of her sophomore year, she chose English, an obvious choice for a future writer. Then in the fall of that year, her life and career at PCW took an unexpected turn.

The academic plan at PCW required liberal arts students to take courses in science, either in physics or biology. Carson chose to take biology and fell completely under the spell of the subject and of her teacher, Mary Scott Skinker. Skinker had come to PCW from New York City, where she had just completed a Master of Arts degree in biology at Columbia University. Skinker was a brilliant and passionate teacher, a dedicated naturalist who was deeply committed to the preservation of rare species of plants and animals. Her passion for biology and the natural world were an inspiration to Carson.

Ever since she was a child, Carson had passionately loved plants, animals, and nature. Until she met Skinker, she had only a limited understanding of how various organisms and their environments were interrelated. Skinker was a zealous ecologist who showed her students how organisms and environments all functioned together. Biology, especially as Skinker taught it, gave a shape and a form to Carson's basic love of nature. Soon it was Mary Scott Skinker rather than Grace Croff with whom Carson was taking long walks about the campus.

"As far as I am concerned . . . there is absolutely no conflict between a belief in evolution and a belief in God as the creator. Believing as I do in evolution, I merely believe that it is the method by which God created and is still creating life on Earth."

—Rachel Carson

Carson began to regret that she had chosen to major in English. She presumed that when she graduated from PCW, she could go on to graduate study in English and eventually earn a living teaching English. This career plan made sense for a woman during the 1920s. A woman who wanted a career in science was at a real disadvantage. Science was considered a man's world. It was generally believed that women lacked the stamina and the intellectual abilities to do well in science. Almost no private company would hire a woman in a scientific capacity. Also, a woman who wanted to teach science could not hope to achieve the same success as a man. She might get a position teaching in a small women's college like PCW, but all the better-known colleges, most of them men's colleges, preferred to hire men.

For a time, Carson wandered the campus in a state of painful indecision while she inwardly debated a change in majors. In January 1928, Carson finally made the decision for science and changed her major to zoology. The sudden switch meant she would have to work hard to make up missed laboratory courses, but she was more than willing to do that.

Carson was devastated when she learned that Skinker had decided to go to Johns Hopkins to do graduate study and would not be around for Carson's final year at PCW. She suffered through a long senior year with a new and poorly qualified female biology professor who had little training in laboratory life sciences and no interest in

Carson sits on the deck of a marine research boat during one of her many trips to collect specimens.

field study. Nonetheless, that year Carson took histology, the study of the structure of the tissues of organisms; and genetics, the passing on of characteristics of living organisms from one generation to the next. She also took classes in embryology, the study of multicellular organisms during their early stages of development. Studies also included organic chemistry and qualitative analysis as well as physics. That spring, Johns Hopkins, one of the most prestigious scientific universities in the country, offered her a full tuition scholarship for her first year of graduate work in biology.

Summer at the MBL

Three weeks after her 22nd birthday in June 1929, Rachel graduated magna cum laude ("with very high praise") from PCW. In the meantime, Skinker had nominated her for a seat at the famous Marine Biological Laboratory (MBL) at Woods Hole, Massachusetts, on Cape Cod. She would spend part of the summer of 1929 at the MBL as a beginning investigator. In July Carson boarded a small commercial passenger boat that took her out of New York harbor on a night voyage up the coast to New Bedford, Massachusetts. It was the first time she had seen the sea. The next morning she transferred to another boat that took her to Woods Hole.

The Marine Biological Laboratory, a branch of the U.S. Bureau of Fisheries, offered summer courses in marine biology. For an eager young scholar like Carson, the MBL was unbelievably exciting. Its library seemed to have everything ever written about the ocean, while its laboratories had all the latest equipment, including seawater tanks, and chemically preserved specimens of a tremendous variety of sea life. Scientists—distinguished scholars and authorities on oceanographic science, some of them Nobel Prize winners—were all around, always willing to talk to a promising young graduate student. And, of course, right next door, within walking distance, was the great Atlantic Ocean.

After graduating from PCW in 1929, Carson took summer courses in marine biology at the Marine Biological Laboratory in Woods Hole, Massachusetts.

Woods Hole had a relaxed atmosphere in which women were encouraged to participate. There were 71 investigators that summer, and 31 of them were women. Every day was different and stimulating. The basic course in elementary invertebrate zoology (the study of animals that lack backbones), was aided by the fact that the MBL used its own collecting boat to gather live sea specimens from the surrounding waters for identification and laboratory examination. Other courses that summer included general physiology, a branch of biology dealing with the functioning of living matter and organisms, marine botany, the study of plants that live in the sea; and protozoology, the study of tiny single-celled lower invertebrates.

It was at Woods Hole that Carson began to store away facts about the sea. Her main task that summer

"Carson was that rare person who was passionately committed when few others believed very much in anything."

—Linda Lear,
Carson's biographer

was to continue research she had begun in her senior year at PCW on the cranial nerves of reptiles. She discovered that no research had been done on the terminal nerve in any reptiles except the turtle, so she decided to compare the nerve's form and function in lizards, snakes, and perhaps crocodiles. She later described those eight weeks that summer at the MBL as the happiest days of her life and Woods Hole itself as "a delightful place to biologize."[8]

Studying at Johns Hopkins University

That September she headed south to Baltimore to start graduate classes at Johns Hopkins. She immediately went back to work on her laboratory explorations of reptilian nervous systems, which she hoped would provide a good subject for the thesis she needed to write to earn her graduate degree.

A month after Carson started at Johns Hopkins, the stock market crashed. This signaled the start of the Great Depression; people began to lose their jobs, and money became more and more scarce. Carson had a summer teaching assistantship in biology, and in the fall of 1930, when the university raised its tuition, she found it necessary to decline her scholarship, become a part-time student, and look for part-time employment. She managed to land a job as a laboratory assistant. This slowed down her work on her graduate thesis on reptilian cranial nerves. The study had not gone smoothly from the beginning. It had turned out to be more difficult than Carson expected to come up with new and useful information.

Reunited with Family

Carson missed her mother and thought she could concentrate better on her studies if her mother would move to Maryland and take over the housework. She suggested that her whole family come out and join her in the house she had rented. In the spring of 1930, Carson's parents left Springdale for good and were reunited with her. Marian and Marian's two daughters arrived in June, and Robert came later.

Carson's happiness at her family's arrival did not diminish her anxiety about completing her master's work in time to graduate. So far, her research on reptilian cranial nerves had failed to yield significant results. Her professor suggested she change her thesis to a study he thought could be completed more quickly. The new thesis proposal was for an examination of the embryological development of what is known as the head kidney, or pronephros, of fish.

Carson followed the professor's recommendation, but the new project also developed complications and took much longer than expected. It was difficult to obtain a series of fertilized fish embryos, and Carson had to search for several months to find a fish hatchery that could supply her with a complete series. When she finally did receive it, she then had to begin the slow and tedious process of dissection, or carefully cutting up and sectioning the embryos for examination and study. Finally, in April 1932, the work was finished and Carson submitted her thesis. Her 108-page thesis was examined and deemed a "worthy contribution" to the knowledge of the urinary system of fish. She received her Master of Arts degree in marine zoology in June 1932.

Carson wanted to go on to earn a doctorate at Johns Hopkins, but her family's health and economic problems made

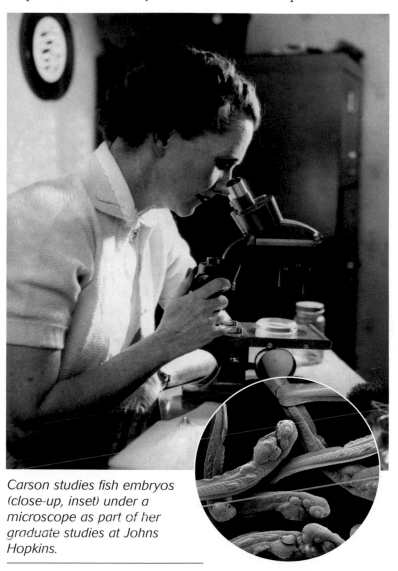

Carson studies fish embryos (close-up, inset) under a microscope as part of her graduate studies at Johns Hopkins.

it impossible. Her sister was diabetic and unable to work. Her father's health was also poor, and Carson found it necessary to support her mother, her father, Marian, and Marian's two young daughters. She gave up her plans to obtain a PhD. She had gotten a low-paying position as a part-time assistant biology professor at the University of Maryland Dental and Pharmacy School. She kept the teaching job and began to search for additional work, but because of the Depression, none could be found. The next few years were a low point in Carson's life and in the economic fortunes of her family. When her father died of a heart attack in July 1935, there was not enough money for a train ticket for her mother to accompany his body back to Pennsylvania for burial.

A Job with the Federal Government

Finally, help came from an old friend. Mary Scott Skinker was employed as a government scientist and encouraged Carson to take federal civil service exams in several zoological areas. Carson scored well on tests for the jobs of junior parasitologist (a biologist who studies parasites such as worms and other organisms that live inside, and draw their nourishment from, the bodies of various animals) and junior aquatic biologist. Skinker urged her to visit Elmer Higgins, chief of the U.S. Bureau of Fisheries' Division of Scientific Inquiry, and ask him for advice about possible employment with the federal government.

Higgins had met Carson previously, just before she started at Johns Hopkins. He remembered her favorably but told her he had no professional openings. At the same time, he let her know he needed a writer for a special assignment—a series of short seven-minute radio shows on the lives of various fish. The series' official title was *Romance Under the Waters*, and it was a challenge to make the series both educational and interesting to the public.

It was an assignment that Carson was ideally suited to handle. She loved writing about anything connected with the sea. At the same time, she was an imaginative writer who knew how to make the subject appealing to a general audience. Carson went home and promptly wrote a couple of scripts.

They were a big success. Higgins's boss was very pleased, and Carson was hired to work two days a week at six and a half dollars per day to turn out 52 episodes.

Freelance Newspaper Writing

Carson used her research on the radio scripts to put together a long newspaper article on the decline of shad fishing in the Chesapeake Bay. The shad was a delicious fish that was no longer plentiful because of overfishing. Carson sold the twelve-page article to the *Baltimore Sun* for twenty dollars. She wrote that the decline of the local fish was "probably the result of destructive methods of fishing, the pollution of waters by industrial and civic wastes and the development of streams for water power and navigation." She ended the piece with a warning that "If this favorite [fish] of the Chesapeake Bay region is to hold its own against the forces of destruction, regulations must be imposed which would consider the welfare of the fish as well as that of the fisherman."[9]

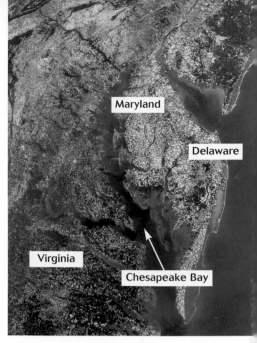

In 1935 Carson wrote an article about overfishing in Chesapeake Bay, shown here in this satellite image.

Joining the Fisheries Bureau

In July 1936, Carson received an appointment as a junior aquatic biologist with the Division of Scientific Inquiry. This new position had been created specifically to assist with the study of the Chesapeake Bay fish and paid $38.48 a week. Carson took the oath of office on August 17, 1936, and became a full-time government scientist, only one of two women then employed in the bureau at a professional level. The bureau conducted studies and collected data on fish populations and also did laboratory investigations of conditions in the bay. In the

In this 1952 photo, Chesapeake Bay fishermen pull in nets full of shad. Carson concluded that regulations on shad fishing were desperately needed.

course of her research, Carson visited bureau laboratories and field stations and analyzed biological and statistical data on the region's fish.

She also consulted with experts in several fields of fishery biology. Her duties employed both her scientific and writing abilities. She did considerable library research as well as laboratory study. On the basis of the data she received and analyzed, she wrote regular reports for the bureau and produced brochures for the public on fish conservation.

A Family Tragedy

Just as her family's fortunes seemed to have improved, Carson suffered a devastating blow in January 1937, when Marian, who had just turned 40, died. The job of raising her two daughters, Virginia, 12, and Marjorie, 11, fell to Carson's mother, who was almost 70, while Carson's task would continue to be to maintain the family finances. Because she needed every extra penny she could raise, nearly every other week she sent a new article idea to the *Sun*. Between January and June 1937, she sold a total of seven articles to the newspaper. Writing these articles and her daily research and writing work with the bureau provided Carson with a great deal of knowledge about the sea and deepened her understanding of the ways in which shore environments and sea environments interacted with one another.

An Article in *Atlantic Monthly*

A year earlier in 1936, Elmer Higgins had asked Carson to write an introduction to a fisheries brochure she had written for the bureau. She called the introduction "The World of Waters." Higgins told her the writing was just too literary for a simple government brochure. He suggested she submit it instead to the leading literary magazine of the day, *Atlantic Monthly*. In 1937, Carson did submit the article, retitled "Undersea," to the *Atlantic Monthly*. It was accepted for publication and she was paid $100 for it. In its "Contributors Column," the magazine told its readers: "Ever since Jules Verne's imagination went 20,000 leagues deep, people have wondered what it would be like to walk on the ocean's floor. Rachel Carson . . . has a clear and accurate idea."[10] Her essay was about the lives of various undersea creatures and the ecological forces that kept them and the ocean itself in balance.

"Successful ideas require great communicators to bring about wide conversion. The single most effective catalyst for environmentalism was an American aquatic zoologist with a sharp pen. . . . If modern environmentalism in the United States had a progenitor, it was Rachel Carson."
—J.R. McNeill, author

Under the Sea Wind

One immediate result of the *Atlantic Monthly* article was a letter from Quincy Howe, senior editor at Simon & Schuster, a New York publishing house. Howe was impressed by Carson's writing and wanted to know if she would be interested in writing a book. Soon after, she sat down with Howe and historian and illustrator Hendrik Villem van Loon. She told them her conception for a book: a narrative account of the lives of three different types of sea creatures—one at the shore, one in the open sea, and one in the deepest parts of the sea. Each creature would struggle to survive and reproduce, and the death of one creature would somehow contribute to the life of another. The ocean itself was the central character.

In November 1940, after three years, the book, entitled *Under the Sea Wind* was finished. It was published a year later in November 1941. Throughout the chapters, Carson has readers experience ocean cycles of night and day, of seasons, and of temperature changes as the forces of the ocean are interwoven with the life cycles of sea animals. In one narrative, she tells the story of snowy owls Ookpik and his nesting mate and their search for food and fight for survival from the ice-strewn sea edge across plains, forests, hills, and valleys of snow. In another, the reader follows the life journey of Scomber the mackerel from his beginnings as an egg in coastal waters to becoming a helpless larva carried by currents to growing into a fish. Scomber's journey is marked by escape from swaying gill nets,

One of the stories in Carson's first book, Under the Sea Wind, *explores the life of a snowy owl.*

huge hungry tuna, stabbing birds, weighted seines, and raiding dogfish until, at long last, the mackerel arrives in the deep quiet waters along the edge of the continental shelf, where he will spend his adult years.

Under the Sea Wind received glowing reviews from major publications like the *New York Times Book Review* and the *New Yorker.* Carson had good reason to wish for a success. If it sold well, it might earn her enough money so that she could quit her job at the Bureau of Fisheries and live out her growing dream to be a full-time writer.

World War II

Five weeks after the book's publication, the Japanese attack on Pearl Harbor on December 7, 1941, plunged the United States into World War II. Suddenly the nation's attention was completely focused on the war effort, and few people were interested in a book about the true life adventures of sea creatures. Carson's book remained on bookstore shelves throughout the war but it failed to sell. By the time it went out of print in 1946, the book had earned Carson only a little over $1,000, a terribly disappointing return for three years of work. She decided unhappily that writing books was not the way to free herself from the routine of her work at the U.S. Bureau of Fisheries.

In the meantime, she had been promoted to assistant aquatic biologist. Her duties, however, were not those normally assigned to someone in that position. She performed only

occasional laboratory work and did not go out on actual field investigation. Her main job was to work on reports generated by others. She performed research, did comparative analyses of the reports, and occasionally rewrote them. Her most important assignment was to produce brochures for the public that were published in a series entitled "Our Aquatic Food Animals."

Early Concern About DDT

As the war came to an end, a series of reports she received began to disturb Carson. They were on the subject of a new synthetic pesticide, dichlorodiphenyltrichloroethane, or DDT. It was a powerful pesticide that had been used with great effectiveness during the war to kill mosquitoes that spread malaria. DDT had saved thousands of military and civilian lives during the war. U.S. troops were protected from malaria when the spraying of South Pacific islands killed the mosquitoes that normally carried the disease. In Italy, a major outbreak of typhus was stopped in its tracks by the spraying of DDT on the insects that carry it. Because of DDT, World War II was, according to environmental scholar Cheryll Glotfelty, "thought to be the first major war in which more people died from enemy action than from disease."[11] Despite its effectiveness, however, DDT was a powerful poison that remained for long periods in the surrounding soil and water and had a devastating effect on wildlife and fish.

Carson was concerned enough to address a query letter to the *Reader's Digest* in the hope the magazine would decide to run a story on the dangerous new pesticide. She wrote:

> We have all heard a lot about what DDT will soon do for us by wiping out insect pests. . . . Experiments [here] at Patuxent have been planned to show what other effects DDT may have when it is applied to wide areas, what it will do to insects that are beneficial or even essential; how it may affect waterfowl, or birds that depend on insect food; whether it may upset the whole delicate balance of nature if unwisely used.[12]

The *Reader's Digest*, however, was not interested in a story about DDT, and Carson turned her attention back to her office work. During the war, the Bureau of Fisheries had become a branch of the U.S. Department of the Interior known as the Fish and Wildlife Service (FWS). By the war's end, Carson had been promoted twice and by 1946 was editor in chief of the division and had a staff of six to carry out assignments. The hours were long and the writing and editing chores often tedious and repetitive. She needed the income but longed to be free to write on her own again.

"Carson introduced concepts relating to the environment and conservation that were virtually ignored by most people during the mid-twentieth century and brought terms such as 'interdependence' and 'the balance of nature' into common usage. She is considered by many to be 'the fountainhead of the modern environmental movement.'"
—Linda Lear,
Carson's biographer

Conservation in Action

In 1946, FWS gave its approval to a plan Carson proposed for a series of twelve booklets. Work on the series, called *Conservation in Action*, took two and a half years, which turned out to be Carson's happiest and most fulfilling time in the FWS. The series informed the public about the importance of the work FWS was doing in various wildlife preserves around the country: waterfowl refuges in Virginia, Massachusetts, and North Carolina, as well as a number of western U.S. refuges such as salmon hatchery fisheries along the Columbia River in Oregon. Carson selected the refuges to write about and approached each one from an ecological perspective. She explained how each of the refuges served certain species of wild creatures by

A deer runs past a large flock of snow geese at the waterfowl refuge in Chincoteague, Virginia.

preserving the natural environments such as wetlands and grasslands the creatures needed for survival.

In a mission statement for the series, Carson noted, "Wild creatures, like men, must have a place to live. As civilization creates cities, builds highways, and drains marshes, it takes away, little by little, the land that is suitable for wildlife. And as their space for living dwindles, the wildlife populations themselves decline."[13]

The Chincoteague, Virginia, waterfowl refuge was part of a chain of waterfowl sanctuaries along the heavily traveled Atlantic coast bird flyway. The refuge provided beaches, dunes, marshes, woodlands, and protected waters for a considerable number of migrating birds. It was established to conserve the greater snow goose and the smaller American brant, which need salt meadows and eelgrass for their winter feeding.

Without refuges like Chincoteague, many birds might not survive their winter migrations. Carson and members of her staff had to personally visit the refuges to do research needed to write the booklets. The assignments gave her a welcome chance to get out of the office and experience nature firsthand.

A New Book About the Sea

While working on *Conservation in Action,* Carson met Henry Bigelow, former director of the MBL and current oceanographic curator at Harvard University's Museum of Comparative Zoology. Bigelow encouraged her to write a history of the sea based on new oceanographic research conducted during the war. By then Carson had recovered from her disappointment over her first book's dismal sales and decided she wanted to write a second book.

Her position with the FWS gave her access to the previously classified government oceanographic information gathered during the war. During the war, amphibious landings and submarine warfare required a thorough knowledge of the effects on ships and submarines of tides, waves, and currents. The navy had consulted with the FWS, and new technologies had been developed to study the ocean. Newly developed scientific instruments included wave recorders that analyzed the origin and speed of waves on the surface and echo sounders that revealed what lay at the bottom of the sea. As a result, a tremendous amount of new information was collected, and Carson planned to make good use of it. In 1948, she wrote to a friend that her new book was "something I have had in mind for a good while [though] I have had to wait until at least part of the wartime oceanographic studies should be published."[14]

Carson saw her new book as a biography of the ocean and wrote: "The book will, I hope, carry something of my conviction of the dominating role played by the ocean in the course of earth history how the very form and nature of our world has been shaped and modified by the sea—how all life everywhere carries with it the impress of its marine origin."[15] Her focus would be on the ocean, but she would not overlook the destruction the human species had brought to the planet in its

In 1948 Carson began working on a new book that celebrated the ocean as the source of all life on the planet.

brief time upon it. Carson strongly believed that as people damaged the land, human dependence on the resources of the ocean would increase in the years ahead.

Carson began work on the new book, entitled *The Sea Around Us*, in 1948. In it, she describes the many parts of the sea: its surface, the sunless floor, the emergence of islands, and tides and how they are controlled by the Moon, the Sun, the winds, and ocean currents. She also describes the hidden mountains and canyons of the ocean deeps and how they were then being mapped; the power of winds, waves, and currents; and the ocean's meaning to humanity—the sea as the giver of all life on Earth.

Because of her job and the complexity of the project, the work proceeded at a slow pace. Carson recalled: "the backbone of the work was just plain hard slogging—searching in the often dry and exceedingly technical papers of scientists for the kernels of fact. . . . I believe I consulted at a minimum somewhat more than a thousand separate printed sources. In addition to this, I corresponded with oceanographers all over the world and personally discussed the book with many specialists."[16]

Deep-Sea Diving

One of the experts with which Carson consulted was Charles William Beebe, the well-known deep-sea diving expert and pioneer. Beebe, who was an expert on the Arctic as well as deep-water oceanography, had in 1930 invented the bathysphere, a heavy steel ball that was lowered on heavy steel cables from a ship into the sea. In 1934, he reached a depth of more than 3,000 feet in the bathysphere. He used it to study and photograph deep-sea life. In writing *Under the Sea Wind*, Carson made extensive use of Beebe's studies and photographs he made during his dives in the bathysphere as well as in a diving suit.

Charles William Beebe (left) poses with his bathysphere in 1934.

Until then, Carson herself had not made any deep-sea dives. Diving, before the invention of portable scuba gear, was not a simple, safe, or inexpensive activity, and few people did it. Beebe told Carson that if she truly wanted to write a book about the sea, she should have the experience of going underwater herself. In 1949, in the Florida Everglades, she managed to go down to a depth of fifteen feet. "I finally got down," she wrote, "under conditions that were far from ideal—water murky, the current so strong I could not walk around [the sea bottom] but hung onto the ladder. But the difference between having dived—even under those conditions—and never having dived is so tremendous that it formed one of those milestones of life, after which everything seems a little different."[17]

Marie Rodell

Carson was still at work on *The Sea Around Us* when she decided she needed a good literary agent. She made some inquiries and chose Marie Rodell, who also became her good friend. Rodell was helpful to Carson in a number of ways. She helped her get a foundation grant that gave her enough money to take time off from her job at FWS and concentrate solely on her writing. Rodell also lined Carson up with a new publisher, the Oxford University Press, and by June 1949, Carson had a contract to complete the new book. Rodell also sent some excerpts from Carson's book to the *New Yorker* magazine, and in 1950, the magazine published condensed versions of nine of the book's fourteen chapters. It was a tremendous boost for the book. The magazine had a large circulation with many influential readers, and the publication of excerpts in advance of book publication helped the book find a much larger audience.

> "*The Sea Around Us* and its best-selling successor, *The Edge of the Sea*, made Rachel Carson the foremost science writer in America. . . . Readers around the world found comfort in her clear explanations of complex science. . . . Hers was a trusted voice in a world riddled by uncertainty."
>
> —Linda Lear, Carson's biographer

A Best Seller

The Sea Around Us was published in July 1951 and was successful beyond anyone's expectations. It sold more than 200,000 copies and was on the *New York Times* best-seller list for a record 86 weeks. It won the National Book Award as the best nonfiction book of 1951 as well as the John Burroughs Medal as the year's best book on natural history.

At the age of 44, after years of obscurity, Carson had suddenly achieved both fame and fortune. She was quite happy with the fortune since she had struggled to overcome severe money problems as the sole supporter of her family for many years. She was not, on the other hand, happy with the fame. Carson was an extremely private person who did not like to be recognized by strangers or pestered to sign autographs.

Yet other benefits helped compensate for the loss of privacy. In 1952, *Under the Sea Wind* was reissued. It soon joined The *Sea Around Us* on the best-seller list. In June 1952, Carson's dream of being a full-time writer was realized and she was able to resign from her job at FWS.

The Edge of the Sea

Carson's next book, tentatively entitled *A Guide to Seashore Life on the Atlantic Coast*, was intended to be a biological sequel to *The Sea Around Us*. The original conception was for the book, like *The Sea Around Us*, to consist of a series of

---

Carson (second from right) appears with other 1952 National Book Awards winners after she was honored for The Sea Around Us.

Carson and illustrator Bob Hines search for tiny seashore specimens in the Florida Keys to include in The Edge of the Sea.

sketches of the lives of various creatures, this time of the seashore. Carson would relate the individual stories of seashore creatures as she had related the life stories of sea creatures in *Under the Sea Wind.*

She began field research in 1951 in Nags Head, North Carolina. In just a few months, Carson and her mother drove 2,000 miles up and down the Atlantic coast. They traveled to Myrtle Beach, South Carolina, and on to the Florida Keys where they met up with Bob Hines, an illustrator for the FWS. Eventually they traveled north to the coast of Maine.

Hines made 160 pen-and-ink illustrations for the book. Many of the drawings were made on the spot. Carson would wade out with a bucket and gather tiny seashore creatures she wanted Hines to draw. She would then bring them to Hines, and when he had finished drawing them, she placed them back in the bucket and carefully returned them to their natural homes.

Hines later described how Carson often forgot all about time during her explorations. She would stand for hours on end, magnifying glass in hand, as she watched in fascination the tiny animals in the icy-cold tide pools of Maine. Sometimes, he recalled, "her body became numb to the point where she had to be carried ashore."[18] Hines, who was a large man, would then pick up the 115-pound Carson and carry her back to the warmth of her car.

Carson made voluminous notes on creatures in four different types of seashore environment: rocky coast, sandy beach, marshland, and coral reef. Carson's reason for writing the book was to show how shore life related to the overall environment of the sea and the land. She wanted to present a selection of animals commonly found in each area and describe the geological origins and the special features of each environment to which they had to adapt. Once she selected the creatures to include, she had to research their life cycles and physical habitats and then show the ways in which they had adapted to different and often constantly changing conditions. Part of her plan was to provide a series of biographical sketches that portrayed the basic conditions of the more important life-forms.

In the course of her research for The Edge of the Sea, *Carson studied the interdependence of such creatures as the heron (bottom right) and hermit crab with their seashore environments.*

Library research was a big challenge. Carson found it necessary to examine thousands of different references in a great many different books. Much of her research was carried out at the MBL library at Woods Hole. Her work was interrupted in February 1952, when her niece Marjorie gave birth to a baby boy she named Roger. Marjorie had inherited the severe diabetes that had killed her mother. Her failing health and the care of Roger as well as the declining health of Carson's mother, then past 80, became major concerns as Carson struggled to continue with *The Edge of the Sea*.

"The shore might seem beyond the power of man to change, to corrupt. But this is not so. Unhappily some of the places of which I have written [in *The Edge of the Sea*] no longer remain wild and unspoiled."

—Rachel Carson

An Ecological Approach

By 1953 Carson was troubled about the structure of the new book. She had a new publisher, Houghton Mifflin, and she wrote unhappily to Paul Brooks, her editor there: "I decided that I have been trying for a very long time to write the wrong kind of book. . . . The attempt to write a structureless chapter that was just one little thumbnail biography after another was driving me mad."[19]

She decided on a different plan—to focus on the lives of the various tiny creatures that make up a tiny tide pool world not as individuals but as part of an ecological community. In his book about Carson's life and work, *The House of Life*, Brooks wrote: "These four types [of shoreline environment] were eventually reduced to three, which—thanks to the configuration and geologic history of the area she was writing about—lent themselves particularly well to the ecological approach, that is, the study of living communities as opposed to merely individual life histories."[20]

The rocky Maine coastline is one of the three distinct ecosystems Carson explored in detail in The Edge of the Sea.

The Edge of the Sea ultimately described three different ecosystems on the eastern coast of the United States: the rocky shore from Maine to Cape Cod, the sandy beaches from there to South Carolina, and the coral and mangrove shores from Georgia to the Florida Keys. As with *The Sea Around Us*, excerpts were published in the *New Yorker*. *The Edge of the Sea* received splendid reviews and became a best seller.

A House by the Sea

With a successful writing career, Carson was suddenly in a position to live wherever she chose. For her, that had to be close to the sea. During the summer of 1946, Carson and her mother first visited the rocky coast of Maine. Carson had fallen in love with the area's wild beauty, and by 1953, she was able to purchase a small summer cottage on Southport Island near Boothbay Harbor. She resided the rest of the year in Silver Spring, Maryland.

In Maine, Carson met Stan and Dorothy Freeman, two neighbors with whom she developed a strong personal bond. Dorothy Freeman quickly became the most important person in Carson's life. The two women had a close friendship and when separated, as they were most of the year since Carson lived in Maine only during the summers, they often wrote one another daily.

Another Family Tragedy

Carson's newfound happiness did not last long. Marjorie's diabetes worsened, and in January 1957, she died at the age of 31. Roger was now in the care of Rachel and her mother, who was then 87 and in need of constant care herself. Carson legally adopted Roger and raised him as her own child. She spent as much time with Roger as she possibly could and took him on nature walks as her own mother had taken her when she had been a young child in Springdale many years before. She never had any children of her own, never seriously dated, and never married. When she was asked about marriage or dating in interviews, she always answered that she simply had no time for such things.

In between caring for an aged mother and a needy young child, Carson struggled to find time to pursue new writing projects. She had written a magazine piece about her nature walks with Roger, "Help Your Child to Wonder," and hoped to turn it into a book. She also wanted to put together a collection of nature writings to be called "Man and Nature." She made additional plans for a short book about evolution. These were all projects she hoped to work on as soon as time permitted. Then outside events took precedence, and Carson felt she had no choice but to respond to what she saw as a dire emergency.

A Lawsuit Against the Government

The nature of the emergency was a campaign of massive DDT spraying carried on in various parts of the country by state and federal authorities. In late May 1957, parts of Long Island were drenched with DDT from the air. The purpose of the spraying was to eliminate the gypsy moth. This was a goal Carson and other environmentalists maintained made no sense to begin with, since gypsy moths inhabited forests and were not found in the suburban fields and gardens of Long Island. The planes swooped down low and sprayed properties repeatedly with DDT mixed in fuel oil—as many as fourteen times in a single day. DDT was inexpensive and the pilots of the spray planes were paid by the gallon rather than by the acre. As a result, they were motivated to spray more than necessary, soaking areas with pesticides.

Marjorie Spock and Mary Richards, the owners of one of the sprayed properties, sued in federal court on the grounds that their constitutional rights had been violated. Another plaintiff in the case was Robert Cushman Murphy, a prominent ornithologist and a friend of Carson's. The plaintiffs charged that land and crops had been badly damaged and great harm inflicted on birds, bees, fish, and beneficial insects. Children and pets as well as domestic animals such as horses and cattle were also endangered.

The trial was due to start in a federal court in Brooklyn in February 1958. Two weeks before the trial began, Carson received a letter from her friend Olga Huckins about the aerial spraying of insecticides over Huckins's bird sanctuary on Cape Cod. Marie Rodell contacted the *Readers Digest*, as Carson herself had thirteen years before, and tried to get the magazine to run an article on the dangers of DDT and pesticide spraying. Once again, the magazine refused, and Rodell told Carson that the *Digest* actually planned to run an article favorable to aerial spraying. Carson then had Rodell contact three other publications: *Women's Home Companion, Ladies' Home Journal*, and *Good*

Carson (left) walks with her niece Marjorie along the seashore in 1955. Marjorie died two years later.

Fish poisoned by DDT are shown in this 1960 photo.

Housekeeping. Not one of the magazines would run an article critical of insecticide spraying. Carson realized that when the country's best-selling writer on the environment could not publish a negative article about aerial spraying, she faced a very difficult struggle.

A New Book

Then, in April, the *New Yorker* decided that it wanted Carson to write a long two-part piece of 20,000 to 30,000 words on the subject of insecticides. By mid-1958, Carson had decided that what was needed instead was a book. In late 1958, she agreed to do a three-part series in the *New Yorker* that would run to 50,000 words, almost the length of a book. At the same time she signed a contract for a book with Houghton Mifflin.

The Long Island lawsuit in federal court provided Carson with a considerable source of evidence and material to include in her book. She interviewed many of the scientists and others who testified as witnesses in the trial and carefully studied and read all the documents relating to the trial. By then, the lawsuit had failed in federal court in New York and the U.S. Supreme Court subsequently refused to review the case.

Carson's Mother Dies

Carson's research was interrupted in late November 1958 when her mother, who was then 87, was felled by a major stroke. A week later Maria Carson died. It was a terrible loss for Carson. The two women had been together constantly for 46 of Carson's 51 years.

A Major Research Task

Carson struggled to overcome her grief and continue with the new book. She had promised to deliver a completed manuscript to Houghton Mifflin by early 1960. She quickly realized that would be impossible because of the enormous amount of research involved in the writing. She waded through more than a thousand documents related to insecticides and interviewed dozens of experts who led her in turn to interview more experts. She knew her research had to be absolutely accurate and impossible to disprove because the moment her book was published, it would come under severe attack from the chemical industry. The use of pesticides had grown from 124,259,000 pounds in 1947 to 637,666,000 pounds by 1960. Chemical manufacturers made tremendous profits as a result—profits they would not want to give up.

Many of Carson's research breakthroughs were the result of the connections she had made with many government scientists and librarians during her sixteen years of government service. Carson hired a research assistant who found evidence of damage caused by DDT as she researched agricultural journals and material in government libraries at various agencies in Washington.

For a time, Carson was not sure where her research would lead her. Author Frank Graham Jr. notes in his book *Since Silent Spring:* "Each piece of information she uncovered seemed to lead to a dozen more. She came to believe that the full horror of the story lay for the most part unguessed at, even by herself."[21] One of her investigations led to an ornithologist at Michigan State University and then to another ornithologist at the University of Wisconsin, who concluded insecticides were responsible for thin and brittle eggshells among breeding birds. The eggshells tended to break, and, as a result, fewer and fewer baby birds were born. Some were born deformed.

Cancer Connection

Another horror Carson uncovered was the link between insecticide spraying and cancer in human beings. She spent long hours at the Library of Medicine and the National Cancer Institute in pursuit of such evidence. From Malcolm Hargraves, a researcher at the Mayo Clinic, she acquired data that revealed a link between chemical spraying and leukemia. Hargraves shared with her the case history of a victim of chemical spraying: "On a hunting trip in Northern British Columbia the latter part of August 1957, we sprayed a tent for twenty-one nights with DDT. We did not sufficiently aerate the tent. When I got back home in September, my marrow and white and red corpuscles were terribly impaired. I nearly lost my life."[22] The man eventually died of leukemia in May 1959.

By the spring of 1960, Carson had made considerable progress toward completing the book, which she had entitled *Silent Spring*. She wrote to William Shawn, editor in chief of the *New Yorker:* "I have a comforting feeling that what I shall now be able to achieve is a synthesis of widely scattered facts that have not heretofore been considered in relation to each other. It is now possible to build up, step by step, a really damning case against the use of these chemicals as they are now inflicted upon us."[23]

Health Problems

Carson was about to send two chapters on the connection between chemical spraying and cancer in human beings to her editor when she found several cysts, a possible sign of cancer, in one of her breasts. Her regular specialist was not available and the usually very careful Carson agreed to be operated on by a substitute surgeon. Following the operation, the surgeon told her the operation had been successful and that she did not need further treatments. In fact, the cancer had already spread. The doctor withheld the truth from Carson because that was a common practice at that time. A doctor often would not share disturbing news with a patient.

That summer, Carson found time to do some campaigning for John F. Kennedy, who was the Democratic candidate for

Young girls at a New York campground in 1946 watch as an official sprays DDT inside their cabin.

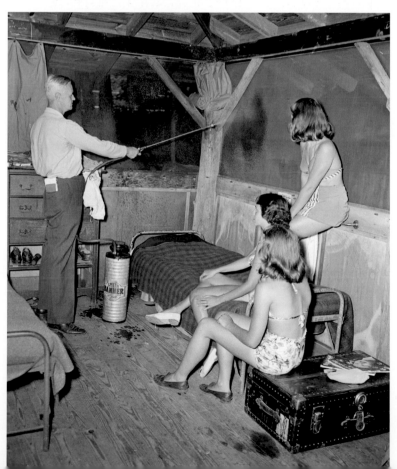

president. She felt that Kennedy and the Democratic Party were more inclined to fight environmental problems than the Republican Party, whose candidate was Richard M. Nixon. That November, after Kennedy had won the White House, Carson discovered a mysterious growth on her rib cage. This time, another doctor confirmed that her cancer had spread and would require radiation treatments. Carson was told that her time might very well be short.

For a time it seemed Carson might not get to finish the book. She felt well enough to attend Kennedy's inauguration in Washington in January 1961, but right afterward, she came down with a serious infection that made it impossible for her to work on the book for five weeks. In addition, radiation treatments for the cancer made her weak and nauseated. On the days when she felt well enough, she managed to get some writing done. Other days, she could only lie in bed and sleep or struggle to deal with the pain caused by the cancer. Then, toward the end of 1961, she was stricken by an eye inflammation. She was in terrible pain, unable to read or look into any sort of light, and for two weeks was almost blind.

"Carson could not be silent. She had peered into the fairy caves and tide pools of her beloved Maine coast and had seen the fragility and tenacity with which even the smallest creatures struggled for life against the relentless ocean tides. . . . She could not stand idly by and say nothing when all was in jeopardy, when human existence itself was endangered."

—Linda Lear, Carson's biographer

No Room for Error
Eventually, however, Carson's health improved. By early January 1962, she was able to work several hours a day with-

out pain and the completion of the book was in sight. Carson knew that she would have to be ready to defend herself and her book against all the attacks that would come. To prepare, she sent copies of her manuscript to many experts in the field and urged them to be as critical as possible and examine her writing closely for mistakes or inaccurate statements. The experts found no mistakes and made almost no suggestions for changes.

Exposing DDT

The book painted a clear picture of the deadly sequence of events that occurred when DDT and other pesticides were used and how they entered the food chain. Pesticides were sprayed liberally on crops and other areas of land, where they killed insects, birds, and often small mammals such as dogs, cats, squirrels, and raccoons. Animals that ate these dead animals absorbed the poisons into their own bodies, where they accumulated in fatty tissues. If these animals were killed and eaten by other animals, the poisons passed into those larger carnivores' bodies as well. At the same time, the poisons worked their way into plant-eating animals. Pesticides washed into the soil. From there they passed into plants that grew out of the soil and were collected in the fatty tissues of animals that ate the plants.

The pesticides that passed through an animal's digestive tract were present in its body wastes, which spread into the soil and then worked down into the groundwater. Some of the poisons found their way into streams, lakes, and rivers and either killed the fish that lived in them and the animals that drank from them or built up in the creatures' bodies. Eventually, if humans ate the contaminated plants, animals, and fish, the pesticides would enter their bodies. Toxins would continue to build up until the humans sickened and died.

DDT was not only deadly but virtually impossible to get rid of. It would not break down under conditions found in nature. A single application on a crop, Carson wrote, continued to kill insects for weeks and months. Furthermore, pesticides killed not only the targeted insects but also countless others, many of

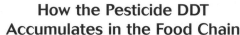

How the Pesticide DDT Accumulates in the Food Chain

1 People spray DDT to control insects.

2 Insects absorb the DDT.

3 Small birds eat the DDT-contaminated insects.

4 Birds of prey eat the contaminated birds.

5 Over time, DDT accumulates in the bodies of birds of prey. This bioaccumulation causes them to lay thin-shelled eggs, which break when they are sat on in the nest.

them actually beneficial to people. Because some of these beneficial insects normally preyed on the harmful insects the pesticides targeted, the use of even more of the dangerous chemicals was necessary.

The Industry Attack Begins

Carson's four long years of hard work culminated in *Silent Spring's* appearance in a series of installments in the *New Yorker*. The first installment appeared in June 1962 and the complete book was published that September. Just before publication, Houghton Mifflin received a letter from the Veliscol Chemical Corporation that suggested a lawsuit would follow if *Silent Spring* were published without changes to negative and supposedly inaccurate statements about the company's products. Veliscol also directly threatened the *New Yorker* with a lawsuit if it did not cancel the last installment of *Silent Spring*. Both the *New Yorker* and Houghton Mifflin consulted with lawyers and refused to cancel or postpone publication.

"As a reporter and a conservationist I see the recent history of pesticide practices and regulation as a problem in communications. The publication of *Silent Spring* in 1962 marked the end of closed debate in this field. Rachel Carson uncovered the hiding places of facts that should have been disclosed to the public long before; she broke the information barrier."

—author Frank Graham Jr.

Veliscol did not carry out its threats to sue, but the pesticide industry trade group, the National Agricultural Chemical Association (NACA), spent well over $250,000 in its efforts to persuade the public that Carson had made errors. It realized that *Silent Spring* could badly hurt the sales of pesticides and cost the members of the association a tremendous amount of income as well as a serious loss of public confidence. They were even more worried about the possibility of new government regulations. As a result, they sought to discredit Carson as a scientist and ridiculed her evidence as well as her conclusions. NACA efforts included the distribution of a brochure entitled "How to Answer Rachel Carson."

The Nutrition Foundation, a research-sponsoring organization of the food industry, attacked *Silent Spring* as a biased and unscientific account written by an amateur. These groups and others attacked Carson harshly because they knew all too well her charges were accurate. Carson's principal biographer, Linda Lear, writes:

> They recognized *Silent Spring* for what it was: a fundamental social critique of a gospel of technological progress. Carson had attacked the integrity of the scientific establishment, its moral leadership and its direction of society. [She] had forced a public debate over the heretofore academic idea that living things and their environment were interrelated. It was the central theme of everything she had written before, and so it was at the core of *Silent Spring* as well.[24]

The most common accusation was that Carson was not a real scientist. Opponents repeatedly pointed out that she did not, for example, have a PhD. She was merely a hysterical female alarmist, they charged, a popular and clever writer, a talented amateur whose appeal was primarily to the emotions of her readers and whose conclusions were not based on careful research or solid scientific fact.

These criticisms were, however, countered by praise from other sources. The most important scientific review of *Silent Spring* came from Cornell University zoologist Lamont C. Cole in the December 1962 issue of *Scientific American*. Cole's review began, "As an ecologist I am glad this provocative book has been written" and was generally supportive of most of Carson's arguments. He differed with Carson on a few points, but ended nonetheless on a highly favorable note: "If the message of *Silent Spring* is widely enough read and discussed, it

In this 1951 photo, farmworkers spray DDT over crops being ravaged by a swarm of locusts.

may help us toward a much needed reappraisal of current policies and practices."[25]

Carson Defends Her Book

Carson did not shrink from defending *Silent Spring*. In late November 1962, exhausted and in obviously failing health, she was interviewed for *CBS Reports* by the highly respected commentator Eric Severeid. Carson made an excellent impression on viewers with her logic and ability to express her ideas. The following April, she was again the subject of *CBS Reports* when it broadcast "The Silent Spring of Rachel Carson." This time, the program presented a variety of viewpoints, including those of government officials as well as a representative of the chemical industry. Three of the show's five sponsors withdrew from the program before it was aired because they feared it was too controversial. Carson was the only expert on the program who was strongly opposed to uncontrolled spraying.

The network estimated a viewing audience of 10 to 15 million people. The television broadcast came at the same time as

Eric Sevareid interviews Carson for a 1963 episode of CBS Reports. *The broadcast introduced millions of Americans to the harmful effects of pesticides.*

the release of a long overdue report by the President's Science Advisory Committee (PSAC). In language that clearly support-ed Carson's evidence, the PSAC report concluded that "the accretion of residues in the environment can be controlled only by orderly reductions of persistent pesticides."[26] It criticized federal government agencies as well as the chemical industry and specifically challenged the government's current pest con-trol program and its entire concept of pest eradication. President Kennedy said he would consider a variety of ways to implement the recommendations of the report and introduce new legislation.

The overall impression the government witnesses gave on the television show was that no one in authority knew very much about the chemicals being used so extensively, nor did they seem particularly concerned about their long-term effects, a point Carson had repeatedly made to her readers. Also, the government witnesses seemed evasive in their answers to the interviewer's questions.

The program was a quiet triumph for Carson and gave her a chance to explain her ecological view of the balance of nature as a series of interrelationships between living things and the environment. At the end of the program, Eric Severed told viewers: "Miss Rachel Carson had two immediate aims. One was to alert the public; the second was to build a fire under the government. She accomplished the first aim months ago. Tonight's report by the Presidential panel is prima facie evidence she has accomplished the second."[27]

Congress and the White House Take Action

The day after *CBS Reports* aired, Senator Hubert Humphrey announced that he had asked Senator Abraham Ribicoff to conduct a broad-ranging congressional review of environmental hazards, including pesticides. Ribicoff would chair a subcommittee of the Senate Government Operations Committee and would hold hearings. Two weeks later Carson accepted an invitation to testify before the committee.

In her testimony, she drew two major conclusions: that aerial spraying of pesticides should be brought under strict control, and that pesticides should be reduced to the minimum strength needed to accomplish the essential objectives. She had several other recommendations, the most important of which was "the right of the citizen to be secure in his own home against the intrusion of poisons applied by other persons. . . . I feel strongly that this is or should be one of the basic human rights."[28]

"Silent Spring . . . is . . . the most revolutionary book since *Uncle Tom's Cabin* . . . the most important chronicle of this century for the human race . . . a call for immediate action and for effective control of all merchants of poison."
—Supreme Court Justice William O. Douglas

Testifiying on the dangers of pesticides before a Senate subcommittee in 1963, Carson urges Congress to restrict their use.

Carson's opponents had already suffered devastating embarrassment and more was soon to come. In November 1963, a massive fish kill on the lower Mississippi River resulted in the deaths of more than 5 million fish. An investigation showed that the fish had died from minute amounts of the pesticide endrin in their bodies. In early April 1964, it was learned that the source of the endrin was a Mississippi waste treatment plant owned by the Veliscol Chemical Corporation, the same company that had tried to stop publication of *Silent Spring* in 1962. As a result of the clear-cut evidence, Ribicoff submitted a draft for a Clean Water Bill while Secretary of the Interior Stewart B. Udall issued a ruling that no pesticide be used if there existed a reasonable doubt as to its environmental effects.

By now, Carson's cancer had spread and she knew that she had little time left to live. She suffered from periodic chest pains and was in constant fear of a heart attack. As the cancer advanced into her bones, the simple act of walking became increasingly painful. Few people were aware that she was dying. When she showed up for a public event in a wheelchair, they were told she suffered from arthritis. She did have arthritis in addition to her cancer, and that explanation was generally accepted.

She received a number of awards near the end of her life. The one that meant the most to her was the Schweitzer Medal from the Animal Welfare Institute. Carson, who was devoted to the rights and welfare of animals, said, "I can think of no award that would have more meaning for me or that would touch me more deeply than this one, coupled as it is with the name of Albert Schweitzer. [He] has told us that we are not being truly civilized if we concern ourselves only with the relation of man to man. What is important is the relation of man to all life."[29]

Rachel Carson's Death and Legacy

Late on the afternoon of April 14, 1964, Rachel Carson died of a heart attack at the age of 56 at her Maryland home. Although she did not live to see it, her work helped inspire important legislation. In July 1964, a federal law was enacted by Congress that required pesticide manufacturers to demonstrate the safety of their products before they could market them. In 1970, six years after her death, Congress passed the National Environmental Policy Act, which established the Environmental Protection Agency (EPA). Today the largest environmental agency in the world, one of the EPA's main functions is to monitor chemicals affecting the environment. Safety standards now require new pesticides to be registered, and the federal government checks pesticide levels in foods to make sure they are safe.

In 1972, the EPA severely restricted the sale and use of DDT. Since 1980, its use has been totally eliminated in the United States

"In 1992, a panel of distinguished Americans selected *Silent Spring* as the most influential book of the last fifty years. Across those years and through all the policy debates, this book continues to be the voice of reason breaking in on complacency."

—Vice President Al Gore

Hatched from DDT-contaminated eggs, these bald eagle chicks would have died if conservationists had not saved them.

and most other countries. DDT is, however, still for sale in Mexico and many third world countries. Linda Lear, in her introduction to the 40th anniversary edition of *Silent Spring*, explains that the export of DDT to other countries around the world has had the effect of "ensuring that the pollution of the earth's atmosphere, oceans, streams and wildlife would continue unabated. . . . Global contamination is a fact of modern life."[30]

In fact, the overall amount of pesticides used on food sources in the United States increased from 617 million pounds in 1964 to 912 million pounds in 1999, an increase of almost 50 percent. Comments Cheryll Glotfelty, "Considering the fact that both in the United States and overseas chemical pesticide use has increased since 1962, it would seem that the lasting significance of *Silent Spring* is to be found in attitudes more than in actions."[31]

Even so, the positive effects of the DDT ban have been significant in the United States. In an EPA report released in 1975, studies were cited that proved the human intake of DDT in the United States had decreased from 13.8 milligrams per day in 1970 to 1.88 per day in 1973. The report also indicated that DDT levels had declined drastically in a variety of fish and birds.

Today, the basic science explained in *Silent Spring* remains on solid ground and has not been replaced by more recent discoveries; instead new discoveries seem to lend more support to Carson's findings.

"Despite the power of Carson's argument, despite actions like the banning of DDT in the United States, the environmental crisis has grown worse, not better. . . . Since the publication of *Silent Spring*, pesticide use on farms alone has doubled to 1.1 billion tons a year and production of these dangerous chemicals has increased by 400 percent."
—Vice President Al Gore

According to environmental writer Norman Boucher,

> The notion that . . . poisons can climb the food chain, becoming more concentrated as they ascend; that chemicals can upset even chromosomes; that pollution can linger long after its source has been eliminated; that chemicals can seriously contaminate ground water . . . these ideas, amounting almost to a summary of today's scientific assumptions concerning pollution are just a few of those first clearly suggested and linked in *Silent Spring*.[32]

Despite the achievement of *Silent Spring*, however, critics past and present have pointed out that Carson herself was not a major scientist and that she did not present any original

Former vice president Al Gore accompanies children during a visit to Carson's childhood home, which today houses an agency dedicated to preserving her legacy.

scientific research. For her own part, Carson viewed her contributions as something much more significant. She wrote to Dorothy Freeman in 1957, "I consider my contributions to scientific fact far less important than my attempts to awaken an emotional response to the world of nature."[33]

Rachel Carson succeeded in those attempts far beyond anything she could ever have imagined. *Silent Spring* remains a milestone of the environmental movement. Its importance was underscored in June 1980, when Carson's son, Roger, then 28, went to the White House to accept a posthumous Medal of Freedom award to Carson from President Jimmy Carter. The award noted that Carson "fed a spring of awareness across America and beyond" and "warned Americans of the dangers human beings themselves pose for their own environment."[34]

NOTES

1. Quoted in Paul Brooks, *The House of Life: Rachel Carson at Work*. Boston: Houghton Mifflin, 1972, p. 232.
2. Quoted in Brooks, *The House of Life*, p. 233.
3. Quoted in Stanley J. Kunitz, ed., *Twentieth Century Authors, First Supplement*. New York: H.W. Wilson, 1955, p. 174.
4. Quoted in Linda Lear, *Rachel Carson, Witness for Nature*. New York: Henry Holt, 1997, p. 7.
5. Quoted in Brooks, *The House of Life*, p. 17.
6. Quoted in Lear, *Rachel Carson, Witness for Nature*, pp. 33–34.
7. Quoted in Lear, *Rachel Carson, Witness for Nature*, p. 40.
8. Quoted in Lear, *Rachel Carson, Witness for Nature*, p. 62.
9. Quoted in Lear, *Rachel Carson, Witness for Nature*, p. 79.
10. Quoted in Carol B. Gartner, *Rachel Carson*. New York: Frederick Ungar, 1983, p. 12.
11. Cheryll Glotfelty, "Rachel Carson," in *American Women Writers*, vol. 1, ed. John Elder. New York: Charles Scribner's Sons, 1996, p. 158.
12. Quoted in Lear, *Rachel Carson, Witness for Nature*, pp. 118–19.
13. Quoted in Lear, *Rachel Carson, Witness for Nature*, p. 132.
14. Quoted in Brooks, *The House of Life*, p. 110.
15. Quoted in Lear, *Rachel Carson, Witness for Nature*, p. 163.
16. Quoted in Brooks, *The House of Life*, p. 111.
17. Quoted in Lear, *Rachel Carson, Witness for Nature*, p. 169.
18. Quoted in Brooks, *The House of Life*, p. 15.
19. Quoted in Brooks, *The House of Life*, p. 158.
20. Brooks, *The House of Life*, p. 159.
21. Frank Graham Jr., *Since Silent Spring*. Boston: Houghton Mifflin, 1970, p. 21.
22. Quoted in Lear, *Rachel Carson, Witness for Nature*, p. 357.
23. Quoted in Graham, *Since Silent Spring*, p. 26.
24. Lear, *Rachel Carson, Witness for Nature*, p. 429.
25. Lamont C. Cole, "Rachel Carson's Indictment of the Wide Use of Pesticides," *Scientific American*, December 1962, pp. 173–80.
26. Quoted in Lear, *Rachel Carson, Witness for Nature*, p. 451.
27. Quoted in Lear, *Rachel Carson, Witness for Nature*, p. 452.
28. Quoted in Lear, *Rachel Carson, Witness for Nature*, p. 454.
29. Quoted in Brooks, *The House of Life*, p. 316.
30. Linda Lear, introduction to *Silent Spring*, by Rachel Carson. Houghton Mifflin, Boston, 1997, p. xxviii.
31. Glotfelty, "Rachel Carson," p. 165.

32. Norman Boucher, "The Legacy of Silent Spring," *Boston Globe Magazine*, March 15, 1987, pp. 37–47.
33. Quoted in Rachel Carson, Dorothy Freeman, and Martha E. Freeman, *Always, Rachel: The Letters of Rachel Carson and Dorothy Freeman, 1952–1964*. Boston: Beacon, 1995, p. 231.
34. Medal of Freedom, "Alphabetical List of Medal of Freedom Recipients from 1946 to Present." www.medaloffreedom.com/alphabeticallist.htm.

IMPORTANT DATES

1907   Rachel Louise Carson is born in Springdale, Pennsylvania.

1925   Carson graduates from Parnassus High School and enters Pennsylvania College for Women.

1928   Carson changes her major from English to biology.

1929   Carson graduates from PCW; she spends the summer at Woods Hole Marine Biology Laboratory; she enters Johns Hopkins University.

1932   Carson receives a Master of Arts degree in biology from Johns Hopkins.

1935   Carson begins writing radio scripts for U.S. Bureau of Fisheries (later Fish and Wildlife Service, FWS).

1936   Carson becomes full-time employee of U.S. Bureau of Fisheries.

1937   Carson's sister Marian dies; Carson's article "Undersea" is published in *Atlantic Monthly* magazine.

1941   *Under the Sea Wind*, Carson's first book, is published; Japanese attack on Pearl Harbor plunges United States into World War II.

1945   Carson attempts to interest *Reader's Digest* in article about dangers of DDT use; *Reader's Digest* rejects article.

1951   *The Sea Around Us* is published and becomes a best seller.

1952   *Under the Sea Wind* is reissued and also becomes a best seller. Carson resigns from FWS to become a full-time writer.

1955   *The Edge of the Sea* is published and becomes a best seller.

1957   Carson's niece Marjorie dies; Carson legally adopts Marjorie's son, Roger.

1958	Victims of DDT spraying bring lawsuit against federal and state governments; Carson begins writing *Silent Spring*.
1960	Carson is diagnosed with terminal cancer.
1962	*Silent Spring* is published.
1963	Carson testifies before two different Senate committees.
1964	Rachel Carson dies at age 56; Congress enacts federal law that requires pesticide manufacturers to demonstrate the safety of their products before they can market them.
1970	Congress passes National Environmental Pollution Act that establishes the Environmental Protection Agency (EPA).
1972	EPA severely restricts the sale and use of DDT in the United States.
1980	The sale of DDT is banned in the United States; it is, however, permitted to be exported to foreign countries.

GLOSSARY

accretion: Growth by addition.

aerate: To let air flow in.

chromosome: A structure in the nucleus of cells of higher organisms that contains an individual's genes and DNA.

corpuscle: A living cell of the body.

DDT: A powerful, long-lasting poison intended to kill harmful insects; also dangerous to other forms of life.

ecosystem: The interaction of a community of plants and animals (including humans) with their environment.

fish hatchery: A place in which humans breed fish under artificial conditions.

groundwater: Water within the earth that supplies wells and springs.

ornithologist: A biologist who studies birds.

prima facie: A Latin term meaning self-evident or "based on first or immediate impression."

FOR MORE INFORMATION

BOOKS

Elaine Landau, *Rachel Carson and the Environmental Movement.* New York: Children's Press, 2004.

Judith Janda Presnall, *The Importance of Rachel Carson.* San Diego: Lucent, 1995.

Arlene R. Quaratiello, *Rachel Carson, a Biography.* Westport, CT: Greenwood, 2004.

Melissa Stewart, *Rachel Carson: Writer and Biologist.* Chicago: Ferguson, 2001.

E.A. Tremblay, *Rachel Carson, Author/Ecologist.* Philadelphia: Chelsea House, 2003.

Ginger Wadsworth, *Rachel Carson, Voice for the Earth.* Minneapolis, Lerner, 1992.

WEB SITES

Rachel Carson Council, Rachel Carson Trust for the Living (http:// members.aol.com/rccouncil/ourpage). Formerly the Rachel Carson Trust for the Living Environment, the Rachel Carson Council is a clearinghouse and library with information at both scientific and layperson levels on pesticide-related issues.

RachelCarson.org (www.rachelcarson.org). A Web site devoted to the life and legacy of Rachel Carson.

INDEX